A HOLIDAY HEIST

KYIRIS ASHLEY

URBAN AINT DEAD

CONTENTS

STAY UP TO DATE

To stay up to date on new releases, plus get information on
contests, sneak peaks and more,
Click the link below...
https://mailchi.mp/6d21003686d1/subscribe

Scan the QR Code below to listen to the Soundtracks/Singles
of some of your favorite U.A.D titles:

Don't have Spotify or Apple Music?
No Sweat!
Visit your choice streaming platform and search URBAN
AINT DEAD.

Currently on lock serving a bid?
JPay, iHeartRadio, WHATEVER!
We got you covered.

Simply log into your facility's kiosk or tablet, go to music and
search URBAN AINT DEAD.

URBAN AINT DEAD

Like & Follow us on social media:
FB - URBAN AINT DEAD
IG: @urbanaintdead
Tik Tok - @urbanaintdead

Submissions

Submit the first three chapters of your completed manuscript to <u>urbanaintdead@gmail.com</u>, subject line: Your book's title. The manuscript must be in a .doc file and sent as an attachment. The document should be in Times New Roman, double-spaced, and in size 12 font. Also, provide your synopsis and full contact information. If sending multiple submissions, they must each be in a separate email. Have a story but no way to submit it electronically? You can still submit to URBAN AINT DEAD. Send in the first three chapters, written or typed, of your completed manuscript to:

URBAN AINT DEAD
P.O Box 448
Maybrook, NY 12543

DO NOT send original manuscript. Must be a duplicate.
Provide your synopsis and a cover letter containing your full contact information.
Thanks for considering URBAN AINT DEAD.

CHAPTER 1

It was the Saturday before Christmas, and Chosen was heading to the mall to finish the last of her Christmas shopping. With Christmas only a few days away, she knew she would have to get everything she needed in this one trip. She hated she'd waited so late to finish shopping, but with school and cheerleading, she had a lot on her plate and just hadn't had the time. Now here she was, rushing to the mall in hopes that she would find everything she needed in the small amount of time she had left before Christmas.

Chosen was the oldest of three girls at sixteen years old. She was followed by her middle sister, Choice, who was twelve and their baby sister, Chase, who was six, all born to their loving parents. Their father, Chance Perkins, was the top jeweler in the state of Michigan. He was the jeweler to the stars and very well-known across the country. Even famous rappers mentioned him in a few of their hit songs. His long hours provided him with a successful career, which provided his family with their every want and need. Their mother, Ava, was a beautiful homemaker who made sure their family was taken care of properly. The two of them together made the dream couple. As high school sweethearts, they'd come from nothing and achieved everything together, even when all the odds were against them.

Chosen slid into her Zara jeans before placing her cream Gucci sweater over her head. Chosen looked exactly like her father, Chance, from his chocolate brown skin and long eyelashes to the deep dimples she had in each cheek. If she hadn't gotten anything else from her mother, however, she'd gotten her mother's wide hips and plump ass. Standing five foot two inches, Chosen had the body of a grown woman at her tender age. She was shaped like one of the women who laid on a table, but hers was natural, given to her by the women on her mother's side of the family. Because of that, her parents had been very overprotective of her, especially her father. Not even allowing her to have boy phone calls until she was fifteen and not dating until she turned sixteen. Even then, her father had to approve of the boy she dated. Growing up, if any of her friends had older brothers, Chosen was not allowed to spend the night at their houses. They would have to come to hers. That rule still stood with her younger sisters as well.

Chance monitored what she wore and enforced other strict rules. Although Chosen had her own car, Chance gave her a ten o'clock curfew that even her mother thought was ridiculous for her age. Sometimes, Ava would let her stay out later on the nights Chance was away for work, which was often. So, most of the time, Chosen really didn't mind. She just wished her father would ease up a bit.

Chosen looked at herself in the mirror as she placed her golden highlighter onto her milk chocolate skin. The jet-black frontal she wore was curled to perfection in a half up half down style, and her gold jewelry was the best accessory for her look. Once she added lip gloss and sprayed her body with her scent of the day, Eillish by Billie Eillish, she was ready to go. Opening her bedroom door, she jumped back when she saw Choice standing right in front of her.

"Girl, why you just standing at my door like that? You scared me!" Chosen yelled out, placing her hand over her chest.

"Sorry, I didn't mean to. I was coming to ask if you could drop me off at Brittani's house on your way to the mall. It's too cold to walk. Daddy not here, and Mama said she had to clean up and finish decorating for Christmas." Brittani was Choice's best friend. She was more like her sister than a friend. They met in the first grade and had been stuck like glue ever since.

Choice had Ava's light skin and long hair. She'd placed it in a bun on the top of her head. Her edges were done to perfection with each baby hair swooped across the top of Choice's forehead flawlessly. Choice looked exactly like their mother with the attitude of their father. She wore a cream turtleneck sweater and a pair of brown leather pants. The one thing they all had in common was style. It came naturally being from Detroit where everyone felt they were a celebrity. No matter what the occasion, the Perkins family was going to dress for it.

"Yeah, that's cool. You ready now?" Chosen asked.

"I just gotta put my boots on. Thanks, Chosen. I'll be right back." Choice ran off down the hallway toward her room.

Chosen made her way down the grand staircase and was met by dozens of opened brown boxes. There were several pieces of garland scattered around the floor, in a trail from the front door all the way to the living room. Three huge piles of lights sat against the wall by the front door. Donny Hathaway's *This Christmas* was playing through the speakers as Ava sat in the middle of the living room floor, pulling out every black and white decoration that was in the box in front of her. Her long, black hair was placed in a low ponytail, and the light gray two piece she wore fit tightly on her body. She wore her usual jewelry, gold hoops, a diamond stud she wore in each ear, four gold chains that hung from her neck, each chain having a C pendent, one for her husband and each of her daughters, and her wedding ring. No matter what Ava wore, she would always have on those pieces. Her light brown skin was flawless without any blemishes, and she didn't need makeup to enhance her beauty. It was their year to host Christmas dinner, and Ava wanted everything to be perfect. With both Chance's parents and her parents flying in from out of town for the first time in years, Ava wanted to make sure she hosted an extravagant Christmas.

"Where you on your way to?" Ava asked, looking up at Chosen.

"I'm going to the mall to finish Christmas shopping, but I'ma take Choice to Brittani's house first."

"I got so much to do. I should have started this shit two weeks ago. Chase was supposed to be helping me, but the moment she finished her hot cocoa, she ran up to her room. I swear, it be yo own kids," Ava joked, shaking her head.

"When I come back, I can help you. I just have a few more things to get, so I should only be gone a few hours."

"Thank you, baby. I know I'm going to need it."

A few moments later, Choice came running down the stairs, letting Chosen know she was ready to go. They both kissed Ava goodbye before walking out the door. The cold air hit Chosen's face as soon as she walked out the door, and she instantly regretted not warming her car before getting inside. As cold as it was, Chosen was only happy there was no snow on the ground.

"What you get me for Christmas?" Choice asked, looking over at Chosen as she started her car.

"Girl, you know I'm not 'bout to tell you."

"Fine. What did you get Denzel?" Choice asked. Denzel was Chosen's boyfriend of the past six months. They met at a basketball game where his cousin played on the opposing team. That night, they exchanged numbers and stayed on the phone until three that next morning. They talked about everything from their family life to their hobbies. Denzel asked Chosen on a date that following night, and they'd been inseparable ever since.

"I'm not sure yet. I still gotta get his gift and Mama and Daddy's."

Pulling out of their driveway, Chosen arrived at Brittani's house a short time later, letting Choice know she would be back to get her in a few hours. She watched Choice walk into Brittani's house before blasting Glorilla through her speakers and pulling off, placing a call to her best friend, Tiara, letting her know she was on the way to pick her up. She pulled up about five minutes later with Tiara walking out the door a few seconds after. She was dressed in a pair of black leather pants, a white turtleneck sweater, and a black leather jacket. Her black hair was parted down the middle and was flat ironed bone straight. The moment Tiara opened the door, Chosen could smell her Burberry Goddess perfume.

"Hey, girl, you ready to get this shopping done? I haven't gotten anything for none of my family," Tiara spoke, smiling over at Chosen.

"Girl, me either. The only person I got gifts for is Chase, and that's cause she the baby. I got her a few toys off Amazon and called it a day. I know I want to get my daddy a watch, but I have no clue what I want to get everybody else."

"What you get Denzel?"

"Girl, I don't know. He a part of the everybody else." Chosen laughed.

"Well, let's get it cause we only got today to get everything done."

They rode, dancing and rapping along to Glorilla's album, *Glorious*, their entire way to Sommerset Mall. They shopped for hours. Getting all the gifts they needed. Going in store after store, they even got a few things for each other.

"I heard my daddy say that he was going on a huge work trip after the new year. He told my mama it would get them both a lot of money. Something about a couple million dollars' worth of diamonds. He said they would be gone for three days," Tiara informed. Tiara's father had been working with Chance for the last five years, and together, they'd brought in millions of dollars.

"I haven't heard anything about when his next trip was, but they always traveling, so what's the big deal?" Chosen asked, confused.

"The big deal is you could use that time to lose yo virginity. If my mama and daddy is gone, that means I will be home alone. You already know my mama goes along with him on all his trips. Yo mama won't care about you staying at my house with me. You and Denzel can have the guest bedroom." Tiara looked over at Chosen and smiled. Chosen had been thinking about giving her virginity to Denzel for the past two months, and now here Tiara was, giving her a way to do just that.

"Girl, I ain't bout to fuck Denzel for the first time with you in the next room." They both laughed.

"My bad, girl. I was only trying to give you a way to lose that V card yo ass still got."

"I get what you trying to do, but I want my first time with Denzel to be special. In a candlelit room filled with flowers and soft music. I want us to spend the entire night showing our love to one another. I really love him, Tiara so much that I want to give all of me to him. I just have to find the right time.

"I get it. Your first time only happens once." They spent the rest of their time finishing up their shopping and finding everything they needed.

CHOSEN AND CHOICE ARRIVED BACK HOME TO SEE THE beautiful white lights hanging from the huge windows of their home. There were two Christmas trees that were visible from the driveway which Ava put up every year. One tree was on the second floor in the balcony window. It was filled with dancing white lights and huge black and white decorations. The main tree was a twelve-foot tree on the main level of the home sitting in front of the huge floor to ceiling window in the living room. Chosen could tell her mother had been working hard at putting up the decorations. She smiled, feeling the Christmas spirit, as she and Choice gathered her shopping bags and headed inside the house.

"Chosen and Choice are home!" Chase yelled the moment they walked through the door. "Are those Christmas presents? Are any of them mine?" Chase continued, running over to Chosen. Smiling from ear to ear and showing off her two missing top teeth, she looked just like both of her parents, taking on the look of the parent she was standing next to at the time.

"No, girl, none of these are yours." Chosen laughed. "Santa won't bring you gifts until Christmas Eve after you go to sleep. But that's only if you've been good."

"I have been good. I've been real good. Mommy making me some more hot cocoa right now because I did such a good job helping her decorate the house."

"Y'all did a really good job, and it's all finished. I'm sure Santa sees what a big helper you've been to Mama," Chosen encouraged. Chosen looked around at the garland that hung from the ceiling covered in white lights and huge black bows. Ava had also twirled garland around the railing of the stairs which was decorated with black bows and white bulbs. The house looked as though it was straight off of Pinterest, and Chosen smiled at the beautiful job her mother had done.

"Daddy said that Santa was gonna get me everything on my Christmas list this year, so I know I've been good," Chase continued.

"Well, that's a good thing. Let me go put these bags in my room then I'll come back down."

Choice helped Chosen take her bags up to her room. Chosen was sure to hide them all inside her closet, being extra careful to not allow Choice to see her gift. Going into her bathroom, she took a quick shower before sliding into a pair of gray leggings and a white t-shirt. After spraying herself with her nighttime fragrance, she headed downstairs with the rest of her family. Noticing they were all inside the living room, Chosen walked inside and joined them on the couch.

"Daddy, can we watch the Christmas SpongeBob?" Chase asked, looking over at Chance with pleading eyes.

"I thought we were watching *This Christmas?*" Choice asked, sucking her teeth.

"We can watch both," Chance suggested, looking from Chase to Choice. Chance loved each one of his daughters equally, and anything they wanted, they got.

Chosen's phone vibrated, and she looked down. Seeing it was Denzel, she answered it, letting him know she would call him back, before she continued spending time with her family. When both movies were over, Chosen kissed her family good night before heading back to her room. Closing her door, Chosen slid out of her sweatpants before climbing up into bed. She turned on her electric fireplace and cuddled under her fluffy, pink comforter before placing a call to Denzel. Although it was close to midnight and she was tired, Chosen knew she wouldn't be able to go to sleep without at least telling him goodnight.

"You going to sleep? It's still early," Denzel spoke into the phone.

"Yeah, I'm tired. I was out shopping all day, then I watched a few movies with my family. I'm lying in bed right now. I just wanted to talk to you before I went to sleep."

"You don't want me to come over tonight and cuddle with you?"

"I do, but my daddy is home."

"Damn, I just knew he was gon' be away on one of his diamond trips. I really wanted to hold you tonight. I miss you, baby," Denzel spoke.

"I miss you too. I wish he was, but he not taking any more trips until after the holidays. But, I'ma see if you can come over for Christmas dinner. My grandparents are coming in town, and I want you to meet them," Chosen revealed.

"You think they gonna go for that? You know Poppa Big Money don't like me too much."

"Aww, don't say that. He don't know you enough not to like you. He just really overprotective of me. Shit, of all us, my mother included. It wouldn't matter who I dated. In his eyes, they never gonna be good enough for me. But don't worry about that. I'll have my mama talk to him. It's Christmas, and I'ma want you here."

"Okay, then I'ma be there."

They ended the call, and Chosen turned on her TV and opened the YouTube app. She went to sleep listening to ASMR every night, and tonight wouldn't be any different. After finding a video to fall asleep to, she watched it until drifting off to dreamland just a short time later.

CHAPTER 2

The next morning, Chosen headed down to the kitchen after smelling the breakfast that was cooking. Ava was at the stove while Chance was sitting at the kitchen island, sipping from a coffee mug. With both her parents being there, she felt it was a good time to ask them about Denzel coming over for Christmas dinner. Greeting her parents, she took a seat next to her father at their black marble kitchen island.

"Good morning, Daddy's girl. How did you sleep?" Chance asked, throwing his arm over Chosen's shoulder and pulling her into a one-armed hug.

"I slept good. I was tired after all that shopping I did yesterday."

"Did you get everything you needed?" Ava asked, taking a pan of cinnamon rolls from the oven.

"Yeah, I'm all done. I'm just gonna chill today. Clean up

my room and do some laundry. I still gotta wrap everything, but I can do that later. I had something I wanted to talk to you and Daddy about though."

"What's going on, baby girl? You know you can talk to me and your mother about anything," Chance encouraged. If nothing else, Chance loved all his girls, and there was nothing he wouldn't do for them. If ever there was a problem or something they needed, Chance would always be there to provide whatever it was.

"Well, I wanted Denzel to have Christmas dinner with us. Since his mom passed away, he's been living with his aunt, and she has to work on Christmas. I don't want him to have to spend Christmas alone, and since we have plenty of room and food, I was hoping he could have Christmas dinner with us." Chosen smiled shyly as she waited for a response.

"Absolutely not! I've already told you to stop talking to that boy. He is not welcomed in my home. You think it's cute to have some little thug ass boyfriend, and it's not. Chosen, you come from something that boy could only dream of, and he ain't going to do shit but hold you back in life. Let it go!" Chance yelled. Chosen could see that he was mad because the little vein in his forehead was popping out with every word. However, she couldn't understand why he was so angry.

"Denzel is not a thug. He's actually a very nice guy, Daddy. And he treats me really good. If you would just take some time and get to know him, you would see that he's a good person. He can't help that he didn't come from a rich family."

"It has nothing to do with him not coming from a rich

family. Hell, I didn't come from a rich family either, but I did what I needed to do to ensure my kids would come from one. You are going places in life that he is going to hold you back from, and I'm not going to allow that to happen. I worked too hard to ensure you and your sisters never have to go through what me and yo mama did. This shit ain't happening. That boy will not be in my home, and you are going to stop talking to him, and I mean that shit!"

"You don't even know him, and you can't tell me who to be with. That's not yo choice. It's mine!" Chosen yelled back before storming out the kitchen, tears streaming down her face. She couldn't believe the way her father was acting, and she didn't understand why.

"I can tell you, and I did. You will no longer have any contact with that boy, and I meant that shit!" Chosen heard Chance yelling out to her, but she said nothing back as she ran up the stairs.

Slamming her room door, she jumped into her bed, crying into her pillow. She was tired of her father trying to control every part of her life. Chosen knew her father loved her, but she would be damned if she stopped seeing Denzel just because Chance told her to. Denzel was the love of her life. He was someone that Chosen saw herself with years from now, and there was no way she would allow her father to come between that. *I don't care if I gotta sneak out every night; I'm gonna see Denzel no matter what he says.*

Hearing a knock on the door, she heard it open as she continued to cry. Looking up, she saw her mother walking toward her. Ava sat on the bed next to Chosen and began rubbing her back.

"Call Denzel and tell him to be here Christmas day at five. Don't worry about yo daddy. I'll handle him. And stop crying. Chance just has to get to know him, and that's what he's going to do." Ava smiled, looking over at Chosen.

Chosen raised her head from the pillow and looked over at her mother. A smile formed on her face, and she wiped her tears before thanking her mother, wrapping her arms around her and hugging her tightly. She knew Ava was going to make everything better. If nothing else, she knew her father would give her mother anything she wanted. So, if she said Denzel was coming to Christmas dinner, that was exactly what was going to happen.

"Come back downstairs and get some breakfast. You wanna come to the grocery store with me to get things I need for Christmas dinner? We can stop at Starbucks." Ava smiled.

"Sure, I just gotta get dressed after I eat." Chosen replied.

Chosen walked down the stairs and into the kitchen. Her father was no longer there, and she grabbed a plate and placed eggs and bacon on it before sitting down at the table. Choice walked in the kitchen a few moments later, greeting Chosen before making her plate.

"You going with Mama to the grocery store?" she asked, taking her seat next to Chosen.

"Yeah, I'ma get dressed after I eat. You going too?"

"Nah, Mama gonna go to twelve different grocery stores and spend all day doing it. I'ma sit this one out. Besides, I wanna clean my room and wrap some gifts. Grandma and Granddaddy coming tomorrow, and Mama wants the whole house spick and span."

Chosen chuckled, knowing Choice was right. Ava would be going to at least four stores in order to get all the ingredients for her Christmas dinner. Chosen knew the routine very well. Ava would start at Kroger before going to Meijer. After that, she would go to Home Goods to get any last-minute decorations she might need. Once that was done, they would head to a restaurant and grab lunch before heading to Walmart. She would end the day at Aldi before heading home. Chosen was ready to accompany her on the entire day just to be out the house and away from her father.

Once she was done eating, she got dressed and went down to the living room to let her mother know she was ready. Chase and Ava were sitting on the couch. Ava grabbed her keys and purse before they all walked out the door.

"You really like that boy, huh? What's his name, Denzel?" Ava asked as she stopped at the light.

"I do like him, Mama; he's a really good person."

Ava nodded her head. She knew all too well what overprotecting a child would do. She knew the more Chance told Chosen she couldn't see Denzel, the more she would sneak off to do so. It was the same thing she did when she was her age and met Chance. Neither of her parents liked him, and they both forbade her from seeing him. Needless to say, Ava didn't allow that to stop her, and about six months later, she was taking a pregnancy test and finding out she was pregnant with

Chosen. As much as she loved her daughter and never regretted having her, she never wanted any of her children to have to go through the things she went through. So, no matter what, she knew she had to ensure that didn't happen.

"He must be if he got you ready to go against your father for him."

"He's not making me do anything. And I'm not trying to go against Daddy at all. All I want is for Daddy to listen to me. He can't judge someone without getting to know them first, and he hasn't even so much as spoke with Denzel. He really cares about me, Mama. Don't y'all want me with someone that loves me and treats me right?"

Ava sighed, thinking that her daughter was too young for love, but she knew she would have to put herself in Chosen's shoes for this conversation. The truth was she had been in her shoes before, and her mother didn't have the same conversation with her. So, she refused to make the same mistake and become a grandmother in her thirties the way her mother did. She wanted better for her children.

"I know how young love can be. You feel like you're in the clouds. But now, you feel like your dad is trying to bring you down from that cloud, but that's not the case. Your daddy loves you, and he just wants the best for you. You're right. We should get to know Denzel, but your father has been a young boy before. and he knows what they want. And most of the time, that's sex. Now, I'm not saying that's all Denzel wants, but you're his daughter. He just wants to protect you. You have to understand that." Ava used her words carefully, not wanting to say the wrong things. She needed to get her point across, but she also wanted Chosen to listen to her and take in what she was saying.

"Mama, y'all raised me to know right from wrong and make good choices. So, now it's time for you both to trust me to make those choices. Denzel is my choice, Mama, and he's a good one. He has never pressured me about sex, and we've been together for months. Denzel loves me, Mama. He loves me the way you would want a boy to love me."

Damn, she really is in love with this lil nigga, Ava thought. The look in Chosen's eyes when she spoke about Denzel was the same look Ava had when she spoke about Chance. Chosen was in love. Ava knew at that moment no matter what she said, her daughter wasn't going to stop talking to Denzel until she was ready. Smiling, Ava ended the conversation, getting out the car before walking into their first store.

They shopped all day, not making it back home until after six that evening. Once Chosen helped her mother put all the groceries away, she placed a call to Denzel to let him know he was indeed welcomed to Christmas dinner.

"I'll be there at five on the dot. You think I should bring something?" Denzel asked.

"Nah, you just have to bring yourself. When my mama hosts for the holidays, that's exactly what she does. Nobody has to bring a thing because Ava Perkins is going to have everything you need on hand. She takes pride in that shit."

"Okay, I hear you. I got you a gift though, so I'll be

bringing that. I'm excited about spending Christmas with you, babe."

"I'm excited too. I'm glad you're coming too. I can't wait to give you your gift. I hope you like it," Chosen spoke.

"I'm going to love anything you give me, baby."

Chosen smiled. She loved Denzel and felt her best when she was with him. From the moment they'd met, she didn't want to be without him. She loved the nights her father wasn't home, and she snuck Denzel in. They would cuddle all night, and he would be gone before her mother woke them up for school the following morning. The love they shared was something she'd never felt before, and she wanted it for the rest of her life. Although they'd not taken their relationship to the next level, she'd been thinking about giving her virginity to Denzel for the last couple of months. She knew it was the most precious gift a woman could give a man, and she felt Denzel was the person who deserved it.

"I know you will, baby, and that's another reason why I love you," Chosen replied.

"I love you too, baby."

They ended the call, and Chosen curled up in her bed, snuggling under her covers. She went to sleep that night with thoughts of Denzel and their future together.

❧

AVA WALKED INTO HER BEDROOM AREA, TURNING OFF THE light in the en-suite bathroom. Chance was already in bed, and he looked at Ava in her black, lace nightgown. He licked his lips as he watched Ava walk closer to him. Removing the covers off him, she straddled him, kissing his neck gently. Cupping her ass tightly, he leaned his head back and moaned softly.

"Damn, baby. You must be trying to get this dick," Chance whispered softly. Without saying a word, Ava positioned his manhood at her opening before easing down onto it. Chance moaned as he entered her wetness. "That's right, baby. Ride this dick fa' Daddy."

"Denzel is coming to Christmas dinner," Ava moaned back.

"Hell yeah, baby. You say you wanna make Daddy cum?"

Ava stopped moving and looked Chance in his eyes. "I said, our daughter's boyfriend is coming to Christmas dinner."

Chance just looked at Ava, knowing that he was about to agree. She knew he would never say no to her while he was inside the pussy. So, he nodded his head before allowing Ava to continue riding him well into the night, leaving him willing to do anything else she said after.

CHAPTER 3

It was Christmas Eve morning, and Chosen woke up early. All four of her grandparents were coming today, and she couldn't wait to see them. She sat on the floor in her room, listening to music, as she wrapped gifts. There was a soft knock on her door, and she ran to it, not wanting anyone to walk in and see their gifts. She cracked the door slightly, seeing her mother standing on the other side.

"We going to pick your grandparents up from the airport. You want to go?" Ava asked.

Chosen shook her head no, wanting to wrap the last bit of gifts she had before placing them under the tree. Each year, her family put on matching Christmas pajamas and had family time before bed. She knew once her grandparents got there, she wouldn't be in her room at all, so this was the only time she had to finish wrapping.

Chosen finished wrapping her gifts and had just placed them under the tree when her mother walked in the door with Chase, Choice, and their grandparents behind her. Chosen ran to them, hugging each of them.

"I missed y'all so much!" Chosen smiled. She spoke to each of her grandparents every Sunday, but it had been months since she'd saw them.

"We miss you too, pumpkin," Nate spoke, hugging his granddaughter tightly. Nate and his wife, Tamika, had been married for almost forty years and were her father's parents. They lived in Chicago in the same house her daddy grew up in. No matter how much he asked them to move into a better neighborhood, they always refused. They didn't care how much money their son had. The house was bought by Nate to be his and Tamika's forever home, and that was exactly what he was going to do. It was a small, three-bedroom home, but it was theirs, and Nate was proud of it.

Although in their early sixties, both Nate and Tamika still acted and dressed young for their ages. Tamika was dressed in a light blue Off White, two piece sweat suit with a pair of all whites. Her long, blonde wig was in a half up half down style with huge curls throughout. Nate matched her fly, wearing the same Off White sweat suit as Tamika. He wore a gold chain around his neck with the same gold pinky ring that he always wore. Chosen had never seen her grandfather without it. Chosen would never say it out loud, but Nate and Tamika were her favorite set of grandparents. Not only did they stay with the latest trends, they were easier going than Ava's parents.

Angela and Philip, Ava's parents, were more reserved. They'd been married just as long as Nate and Tamika had, but they lived a much different lifestyle. They lived in a four bedroom home in the suburbs of Chicago, and although they weren't rich, they lived a comfortable life without the help of anyone else. Angela wore a pair of black slacks with a white silk button up shirt. Her hair was in a short pixie cut, and she wore diamond studs in her ears. Philip wore a pair of jeans and a Chicago Bulls sweatshirt.

"You all ready for Christmas, baby girl?" Philip asked.

"Yep, I just finished putting the gifts I brought under the tree."

"Okay, I might have a little something for you in my bag. It depends on if Santa calls me and tells me you girls have been good this year," he joked.

"I been real good, Granddad, so I know Santa gonna tell you that," Chase chimed in.

"Okay, we shall see on Christmas morning."

"Come on, Granddaddy. I'ma show you and Grandma to y'all room," Chase informed, grabbing Philip's hand.

"G mommy and Papa, y'all stay right here, and I'll be right back. Mommy told me it was my job to show y'all rooms to y'all, and that's what I'ma do. Santa gonna see I'm a real good girl and bring me lots of gifts." Chase smiled before taking them down the hall to the guest room they would be staying in.

"Do we need to go to the liquor store? You know I need my wine," Tamika asked, looking over at Ava.

"Nah, we good on all that. I went to the store the other day, and I got wine and liquor. We ain't gonna have to go to no stores for nothing the entire time y'all here," Ava replied.

"That's what I'm talking 'bout. I knew I could count on my favorite daughter-in-law to have my back."

"What you talkin' 'bout, Tamika? I'm your only daughter-in-law."

"And that's why you my favorite." Tamika laughed.

Chase ran back to them a few moments later, taking Nate and Tamika upstairs to the room they would be staying in. About an hour later, everyone met in the living room in their Christmas pajamas. Chance pulled out a Christmas murder mystery game. They all had a good time acting out the characters and finding out who the true murderer was. When they were done, they baked cookies and popped popcorn. Chase put away some cookies for Santa before they all took the rest of the cookies and popcorn back into the living room. They all set on the couch and watched *Home Alone*.

When the movie went off, Chase and Choice went up to Choice's room for the night. They usually watched Christmas movies until they went to sleep. Chosen stayed up a few more hours, helping her mom and grandmothers in the kitchen. Her mother was making a huge feast and needed all hands on deck helping her prep the night before.

"Ava, I think it's time for you to break out a little drink.

I'ma need something if you want me to stay up. Shit, I already been up since five this morning," Tamika suggested.

"I was thinking the same thing." Ava laughed. "What you want? Wine or tequila?"

"Girl, give me some of that tequila. You got a little lime juice or lemonade?"

"You know I got you." Ava nodded, grabbing the liquor and juice from the refrigerator. "You want a drink too, Mama?"

"Nah, I don't want none. Y'all gonna be too hungover to get up with them kids tomorrow to open gifts. I'm gonna see my grand babies smiling faces in the morning. Even if the rest of y'all are laid out drunk." Angela shook her head.

"Girl, shut up. It's Christmas Eve, and you still acting like a bitch? Take this drink and lighten the hell up. Hell, pour yo husband one too. Maybe then he can hit that shit right. Ain't no way a bitch getting good dick is this mean."

Both Chosen and Ava's mouth fell open, not believing the words that had just come from Tamika's mouth. Over the years, there had always been a feud between the two. With it being the worst up until Chosen was about two years old. Although it had calmed down over the years, they still threw shots at each other from time to time.

"My husband knows exactly what he's doing. Thank you. But I will take that drink, Ava. I'm going to need something to get me through three days of being in the same house with this hoodrat."

Ava shook her head, placing three glasses on the table and pouring liquor and juice into one before Tamika and Angela did the same. Once everything was done and Chance had put all the gifts under the tree, everyone went to their rooms for the night.

CHAPTER 4

The entire family sat in the living room opening the many gifts that were underneath the tree. The curtains were opened, showing the huge flakes of falling snow, and the fireplace was lit. Black and white wrapping paper was scattered across the living room floor. No matter how many times Ava asked Chase to put the wrapping paper into garbage bags, her excitement was just too much. Chance and Ava made sure to get each of their children everything they asked for on their Christmas lists and more. They'd even gotten each of their parents very expensive gifts they all loved. Everyone was all smiles.

Once all the gifts were opened, Ava went into the kitchen with Angela and Tamika to begin cooking Christmas dinner. Most of it was prepped the night before, so they didn't have much to finish. Chance set on the couch with Nate and Philip watching TV, while Choice and Chase sat on the floor going through all the gifts they'd gotten.

Chosen had taken all of her gifts up to her room and was now putting all of her clothes and shoes into her closet. She'd already had an outfit she'd bought to wear for dinner. However, now that she'd seen the items she'd received, she was now rethinking her choice. With Denzel coming over for dinner, she wanted to look perfect, and she knew that started with the perfect outfit.

She'd just put everything away when her cell phone started ringing. Walking over to her nightstand, she picked it up before noticing it was Denzel. Smiling, she answered.

"Merry Christmas, baby!"

"Merry Christmas, boo. Are you all done opening your gifts?" Denzel asked.

"I actually just finished putting everything away. I can't wait to see you and give you one of your gifts."

"One of them?" Denzel asked, confused.

"Yeah, I can only give you one today. The other one will have to wait until my daddy goes back to work."

"Oh, is that right?" Denzel questioned. Chosen could hear him smiling from over the phone, and she knew he knew exactly what she was referring to.

Chosen had decided that she would indeed give her virginity to Denzel. However, she was going to do it the way she wanted. Although she appreciated Tiara's offer to use her guest room, Chosen just couldn't take her up on it. Chosen wanted her first time to be special. She'd never felt the way she felt for Denzel about anyone. The love she had for him was real, and Chosen thought they would be together forever. So, with that, she made the choice to give her body to him for the first time. Her mother had always told her to wait until she found a man that would appreciate such a precious gift. There was no other man Chosen thought was more deserving of it than Denzel. He would place the entire world in her hands if he could, and Chosen knew that. So, it could only be Denzel that she gave herself to.

"You just wait until he goes back to work. I'm going to give you the best gift of your life."

"Man, wish that nigga would get called into work tonight," Denzel joked.

They both laughed, conversing for a few more moments before ending the call. Walking into her en-suite bathroom, Chosen showered with her vanilla scented body wash before rubbing herself down with EOS vanilla cashmere lotion. She slipped into the pink Versace robe she was gifted from her father before walking back into her room. Turning on her playlist and hooking her phone up to her Bluetooth speaker, Sza began singing, and Chosen took a seat at her vanity. Her grandma, Tamika, had gifted her with a new forty-inch full lace unit that she planned to install today. She knew the hair would go great with whatever she decided to wear. She placed six braids in her hair before placing a wig cap onto her head and gluing it down with got2b spray.

After gluing the wig onto her head, she placed a band across her lace before styling her hair. Once Chosen applied her makeup, she slid into a pair of chocolate brown, leather pants, a caramel brown sweater, and her chocolate brown, Givenchy shark boots. One thing about it, Chosen didn't give a damn what Latto said. She was going to wear her shark boots. After placing the gold Fendi jewelry and spraying herself with Valentino Donna Born in Roma Intense, she headed downstairs. Walking into the living room, she saw her father and grandfathers still sitting on the couch, watching the game.

Walking into the kitchen, she saw her mother and Grandma Angela putting the finishing touches on dinner. With them not needing any help, Chosen decided to help her G mommy, Tamika, set up the food table. Walking into the dining room, she saw Tamika placing serving spoons atop of small black plates. She was dressed in a long, form-fitting, black dress. Her hair was now in a bob, and the matte red lip she rocked made her look at least ten years younger.

'I hear you have someone special coming to Christmas dinner." Tamika smiled as she looked over at Chosen.

"Yeah, and I can't wait for y'all to meet him. He's everything, G mommy."

"I see. I can see the sparkle in your eyes when you talk about him. Young love is a beautiful thing. You just better make sure he keeps treating you right. The second he starts to switch up, you remind that lil nigga why you that girl. And don't be giving up the cookie too soon either. You still got yo V card?"

"G mommy, don't say that." Chosen laughed. "But yes, I'm still a virgin."

"Good, keep it that way. If he really the one for you, he will wait for you without any pressure. It's yours to give, so you wait until you're ready to give it."

Chosen nodded her head, taking in everything Tamika was saying to her. It was almost as if Tamika was reading Chosen's mind, and that was why she loved her so much. Tamika would always be there to give her the game straight how it was, and Chosen would always respect her for that. The doorbell chimed, and Chosen ran to the door, already knowing who it was. Opening the door, she jumped into his arms, greeting Denzel with a kiss. He had a huge gift bag in his hand which he handed to Chosen.

"Thank you, baby." She smiled, taking his hand and leading him inside the house. She walked him inside the living room where her dad and grandfathers sat.

"Hey, y'all. I want y'all to meet somebody. This is my boyfriend, Denzel. Denzel, this is my daddy, Chance Perkins. This is my papa. Mr. Perkins, and my granddaddy, Mr. Kirkland," Chosen introduced, pointing out each man.

"It's nice to meet you all," Denzel spoke, walking up to each man, shaking their hands.

"Its nice to finally meet you too, young man. I"ve heard you and my daughter have been friends for some time now, but this is the first time we've formally met." Chance spoke.

Chosen cut her eyes at chance not wanting him to take the conversation any further. Chance knew full well why this was the first time he was meeting Denzel and Chosen wasn't going to allow him to spin it any other way. Chance, noticing the look Chosen was giving him, smiling. Lightening is tone and demeanor.

"Come on. Let's go into the kitchen, so you can meet my mama and grandmothers. They in there finishing up dinner," Chosen suggested.

Denzel nodded his head, taking Chosen's hand and following her. Chosen had never been happier. Out of all the gifts she'd received that day, her most valued possession was standing right beside her. Once Denzel had been introduced to everyone, Chosen took him into the den, so they could exchange their gifts in private.

"Have a seat on the couch. I gotta run to my room and get your gift," Chosen suggested before walking off. She returned a few moments later with a box she'd wrapped neatly in black and white checkered wrapping paper. She handed the gift to him, and Denzel allowed Chosen to open her gift first.

"Open the big one first," he requested.

Reaching into the gift bag, Chosen pulled out the largest of the two boxes that were inside and opened it. Inside was a soft pink blanket with a picture of her and Denzel on the front of it.

"OMG, I love it, Denzel. Thank you! I'm going to sleep under it every night."

"I'm glad you like it, baby. Go ahead and open the other one."

Chosen smiled, reaching back into the bag, excited to see

the next gift. Pulling the small box from the bag, she opened it to see a beautiful gold heart shaped necklace. There were diamonds all around it with a picture of her and Denzel in the middle. Wrapping her arms around him, they kissed passionately as she thanked him for her gift. *I know this necklace cost him hundreds of dollars that I know he didn't have. Damn, I love him.*

"It's your turn now, baby. I hope you like it," Chosen spoke, handing the box over to Denzel.

"I'm going to love anything you got me." Denzel tore through the paper until it was just a plain white box in front of him. When he saw the Cartier box, his eyes lit up, already knowing what was inside.

"Aw, baby you got me some buffs? These shit's dope as fuck." Taking them out the box, Denzel placed the brown tinted frames on his face before kissing Chosen.

"I'm glad you like them."

"I love them, baby."

Just then, they heard Ava calling out to everyone, letting them all know dinner was ready. Chosen grabbed Denzel's hand and led him to the dining room. Ava set the table to match the Christmas décor, so everything was black and white. There were two small, white Christmas trees with black gifts underneath them as centerpieces. The placemats were huge, white snowflakes, and a stack of black plates set atop of each one. There was a separate table in the corner of the room that housed the spread that had been prepared with all the food sitting in black serving trays. They all stood around the table, grabbing hands, as Chance blessed the food.

"You want me to make your plate?" Chosen asked, looking over to Denzel. However, before he could answer, Chance spoke.

"I'm sure his hands work, so he can make his own plate."

"Daddy!" Chosen yelled out in embarrassment.

"Calm down, Chance. I'm sure Chosen was just being polite. After all, Denzel is a guest in our home."

"Mommy makes your plates, Daddy," Chase chimed in.

"It's okay, Chosen. Yo daddy is right. I can make my own plate." Denzel picked up a plate from the table and followed Chosen over to the food table, filling his plate with all the items he wanted to try.

"Be nice to him, Chance. Your daughter likes him," Ava whispered once Chosen and Denzel walked away from the table.

"I don't care. I can see right through that lil nigga."

"Be nice to him and I'll be nice to you tonight."

"You always know how to get me." Chance laughed.

"We call that the power of the pussy." Ava smiled.

Once everyone's plate was made, they all sat around the table, enjoying the meal that had been prepared.

"How long have you known Chosen?" Philip asked, taking a bite of a turkey wing.

"We met a little over six months ago at one of her school games."

"Oh, so you two go to school together?" Nate asked.

"No, my cousin was playing on the team her school played. I was just there to support him," Denzel replied.

"What school do you go to?" Tamika asked.

"I go to school online."

"Online? Why don't you go into a building and learn like all the rest of the kids?" Philip asked, looking over at Denzel for an answer.

Denzel put his head down, trying to get the words out to answer the question. Chosen, feeling his sadness, grabbed his hand. She intertwined her fingers in his before answering for him.

"After the loss of his mother, Denzel moved in with his aunt and decided it best to attend online school while doing so."

"I'm sorry to hear about your loss, Denzel," Tamika spoke.

Everyone at the table extended their condolences with Denzel thanking them.

"Denzel, where do you see yourself in ten years?" Chance asked, changing the subject.

"Honestly, I just see myself making a beautiful life for me and Chosen." Chosen smiled as she looked over at Denzel, knowing his words were true.

"How do you see yourself doing that? What career do you want to have that would provide my daughter a comfortable life?" Chance asked.

"Honestly, I'm going to do whatever I got to do. Right now, I have a YouTube channel that's growing everyday. I also make T-shirts that I sell. I'ma do anything I can do to make sure Chosen is taken care of," Denzel replied.

"Oh, so you're an entrepreneur. I like that. Keep poppin' yo shit," Tamika encouraged, raising her wine glass up to Denzel.

"Thank you, Mrs. Perkins."

"Do you have a backup plan? You know, just in case that plan doesn't work?" Philip asked.

"Naw, I don't. I don't believe in backup plans. If you have a backup then you already planning to fail. There's no failure in my blood."

"I like that. This boy has a good head on his shoulders," Nate complimented.

Chosen smiled as she thanked him. She couldn't have been prouder of Denzel. He was standing his ground with her family, and he was doing it respectfully. She wanted to plant the biggest kiss on his lips, but she knew no one at the table would approve of that, so she kept her composure. They continued sitting around the table, eating and conversing, enjoying the meal and each other.

CHAPTER 5

"Dinner was delicious. Thank y'all for having me." Denzel expressed his gratitude. This had been the best Christmas he'd had since his mother passed away, and he couldn't have been more thankful to have Chosen in his life.

"You're welcome. Any friend of my children is always welcomed at our home. I hope you saved room for dessert. We have a lot to choose from," Ava replied, standing to her feet and walking into the kitchen to roll out the dessert tray. She'd just made it back to the dining room when the doorbell chimed.

"Whoever is at the door is late for dinner," Tamika joked, sipping from her glass of red wine.

"We're not expecting anyone else," Chance informed, standing from his seat at the head of the table. Chance walked toward the door, looking out the peephole. There was a tall, white man with short, blonde hair standing there in a FedEx uniform, holding a tablet in one hand. Chance thought it was unusual seeing how it was Christmas day, but he spoke over the intercom anyway.

"Can I help you?"

"I'm sorry to bother you on Christmas, sir, but a very important package was delivered here. I just need to get it to the right house," the man spoke, looking up at the door. Chance wasn't aware of any of the packages that came to the house other than there were a lot of them. His wife and daughters had packages coming everyday leading up to Christmas, so it would be very possible.

"What's the name on the package?"

Chance watched as the man looked down at the tablet before replying. Chance let him know he would ask the rest of his family before walking away from the door.

"Does anyone know about a package coming for a Daniel Coleman?" he asked, walking back into the dining room.

"Nah, I haven't seen any packages coming for anybody that doesn't live here," Choice answered.

"Yeah, me either," Chosen responded.

"Is the guy sure his package came here?" Ava asked.

"Yeah, it's FedEx at the door, and the guy said it was delivered here."

"FedEx? It's Christmas day, Ain't no delivery drivers out today," Tamika spoke.

"Well, I guess it is because it's one at the door right now. I'll just tell him it's not here. I'll be right back." Chance walked back to the door, looking out the peephole and seeing the man still standing outside looking down at his tablet. Pressing the intercom button, Chance let the man know the package wasn't there.

"Can you just sign this stating I was here? The last thing I need is for them to be trying to say I stole the package. The manager bet his life that it was sent to this address, and I'm not trying to get fired coming back empty handed."

Chance understood, not wanting the guy to get fired. He disarmed the alarm, unlocking the door and opening it. The moment he opened the door, three masked men rushed in with guns, pushing Chance to the floor.

"Run!" he yelled before one of the men hit him in the face with his gun.

Ava, hearing her husband yelling, rushed toward him. Seeing a man standing over him with a gun, she screamed before turning around and rushing toward her children, yelling for them to get up and run to the side door, only to be yanked back by her hair. Choice immediately grabbed Chase and ran toward the door. Chosen did the same with Denzel right behind her. Both Philip and Nate ran toward the living room to see what was going on only to be halted by two men holding guns in their faces.

Choice and Chase made it to the back door first but stopped, allowing Chosen and Denzel time to catch up. They were all scared, not knowing what to do. Denzel whispered that he would open the door. He didn't know what was going on, but he knew he needed to protect his girl and her sisters.

Placing his hand on the doorknob, he turned it slowly. However, as soon as he opened it to step out, he was hit in the face so hard that he was knocked to the ground.

"Ahhhh!" Chosen screamed as she watched Denzel fall to the floor.

Choice, thinking quickly, grabbed Chase and took off running down the hall before whoever was coming in the door saw them while Chosen bent down, attempting to help Denzel to his feet. A woman stood there in all-black with thigh high, leather boots, now pointing a gun on the both of them. She had a black mask covering the bottom of her face, and her long, jet-black hair was parted down the middle.

"Get the fuck up and walk," she ordered.

Denzel stood to his feet, placing Chosen behind him. Blood poured from his nose, and it hurt so bad that he knew it was broken. Still, he stared the woman in her eyes,

"Don't try and be no Captain Save a Hoe. Start walkin', muthafucka," she reiterated, pointing the gun down the hallway.

If this bitch didn't have that fuckin' gun, I know I could take her and get me and my baby outta this shit, Denzel thought, taking Chosen and walking back down the hallway. He didn't know where Choice and Chase went. He just hoped they'd gotten away and was now off getting some help.

"Okay, got it," they heard the woman say.

Denzel turned around to see who she was talking to, but she quickly told him to turn back around and take her to the living room. Denzel knew then that she must've been speaking through an earpiece. He could feel Chosen's hand shaking inside his, and no matter what they faced when they walked into her living room, he knew he wasn't going to allow any harm to come her way.

They walked inside the living room to see all the adults sitting on the floor against the wall as a masked man held a gun on all of them. Although they couldn't see his face, he was buff with huge muscles and seemed to be a bit shorter than the other two men. There was another masked man standing in the corner of the room, whispering to someone on the phone. Denzel couldn't hear what he was saying, but he could tell he had a deep voice. There was another guy who seemed to be the tallest of all the men. He was looking around the room at all the family photos, Chosen ran over to her mother and father, still holding Denzel's hand. They sat between them with Denzel sitting next to Chance and Chosen sitting next to Ava.

"Where is Choice and Chase?" Ava whispered into Chosen's ear.

"I don't know. They ran off when we got stopped at the door. I hope they got away and went to go get help," Chosen recalled.

"Ain't no whispering, little girl, If you got something to say, you say that shit in front of everyone," the shorter man spoke out, walking over to Chosen and kneeling down in front of her.

"Don't you talk to her. She is a child! My child!" Chance yelled out, scooting in front of Chosen as Denzel placed his arm around her. They both were there to protect her with their lives, and they wanted everyone to know it as they both stared the man in his eyes.

"Hahaha," The man laughed. "Calm down, Nobody is here to hurt anyone. We just need to make sure y'all stay out the way. First things first, is there anyone else in the house?"

"No!" Ava quickly answered. She didn't want to take the chance of anyone telling the intruders about Choice and Chase.

"Go check the rest of the house," Short Man spoke to Tall Guy. He nodded his head, pulling his gun from his waistline before walking down the hallway. Angela looked over to Ava as if to ask, *Where is Choice and Chase?* but Ava shook her head quickly, not wanting anyone else to notice.

"Please just take what you want and leave us alone. We won't say anything, just don't hurt us," Ava pleaded.

"Like I've said before, we're not here to hurt anyone. We're only here for the diamonds. After that, we will be on our way," Short Man spoke. "I'll have you show me to the safe when my colleague has finished clearing the house."

"He better hurry up. We been here for three minutes already," Deep Voice informed.

"It's cool. We got it. Soon as he gets back. Mr. Diamond here is gonna show me to the safe, and we out."

"I don't know why you think there is a safe here with diamonds inside, but I'm sorry to tell you that it's not. You must have the wrong house," Chance responded.

Ava looked over at him when he spoke those words. She

didn't know why her husband was lying. She'd seen him put a bag of diamonds in the safe herself just two days ago. She also knew if they were in their house for diamonds then they knew they were there.

"Hahaha, see here you go." Short Guy pointed his finger at Chance. "Please let's not do that. We here because we know all about you. We know who you are, Chance Perkins, so we know diamonds come behind that name. We want this to be easy and so should you. Just give up the diamonds, so you can go back to Christmas dinner with yo family."

"There are no diamonds here!" Chance said once more, this time yelling. His mind was racing because he had no clue who these people were. Although he knew a lot of people might know of him, there was only a select few that knew where he lived, and even fewer knew about the safe he had inside his home. He knew this had to be an inside job; he was just unsure who.

Having heard enough of his lies, Short Man took his gun and hit Chance in the face with it. Nate jumped to his feet, yelling at the man, but was quickly silenced when he hit Nate in the face with the same gun, causing everyone to yell out in his defense. Tamika rushed over to her husband, using her body to shield him from any more blows as she helped him back against the wall.

CHAPTER 6

Choice and Chase ran through the halls as quickly as they could, trying not to get caught. Choice didn't know what was going on, but she knew she had to get her and Chase out safely and try to get help for the rest of their family. She'd left her iPhone at the dinner table, so she couldn't call for help. Her best bet would be to run to a neighbor's house. However, she didn't know how they would get out the house.

Running up to the third floor, they ran down the hall until they got to the family library. Opening the door and quickly walking inside, she closed it behind them. Running up the stairs, they went up to the loft area and hid behind the couch. Choice's heart beat fast, and her palms sweated. She didn't know what her next move was going to be, but when she looked down at Chase's tear-filled eyes, she knew she had to do something.

"Don't cry, Chase. Everything is gonna be okay. We just have to figure out a way to call for help. Do you have your phone on you?"

"No, it's in my room." Chase shook her head. "I had so many new toys to play with, I wasn't even thinking about my phone," Chase replied.

Choice nodded her head in understanding. She wracked her brain trying to think of another strategy. She knew the longer they sat there and waited, the less likely it was that her entire family would survive.

"Chase, if I leave you here, can you be a big girl and stay hidden until I get back?"

"No, please don't leave me, Choice. I'm too scared. What if they come in here and you not here? I don't want them to get me," Chase cried.

Choice nodded her head, knowing her sister was scared. She was scared too, but she knew she was the only one that could make a move for her family. She needed to get to a phone and at least call for help. She was just about to open her mouth to speak when she heard the door to the library open. Placing her finger to her lips, she signaled for Chase to stay quiet. Crawling slowly to the end of the couch, she looked down to see who'd walked into the room. Her heart dropped when she saw the masked man in all black.

"One of them are in here," Choice mouthed, looking back at Chase. More tears began to fall down Chase's cheeks, and Choice placed her finger over her lips once more. Chase nodded her head and quickly wiped the tears from her face.

Choice watched as the man looked around the room a few more times before walking out the room, closing the door behind him.

"He's gone," Choice whispered, crawling back toward Chase. "We'll wait a few minutes before we go to your room and get your phone."

✦

"Phones now!" the short man ordered. Chance, Nate, and Philip all reached into their pocket and pulled out their phones before handing them off to him with Chosen and Denzel doing the same. Tamika reached down in her bra and pulled out her phone before handing it off as well. He waited for a few seconds before holding his gun up, pointing it from Angela to Ava. "I said give me your fucking phones!"

"My phone is in the dining room," Angela replied, holding both hands up in surrender.

Turning his gun on Ava, she informed him that her phone wasn't on her. As if he didn't believe her, he grabbed her arm and pulled her to her feet. She screamed as he pulled her closer. Chance, wanting to protect his wife, stood to his feet, but the taller man walked in the room just in time to pull his gun on Chance, stopping him from going any further.

"Seven minutes," Deep Voice spoke.

Without saying a word, Short Man began patting Ava down, searching for a phone. When he didn't come up with one, he tossed Ava back to the floor.

"I found these in a few of the rooms when I searched the house," Tall Guy announced, holding up three phones.

"You, Mr. Diamond Dealer is going to show me to that safe, so we can get what we came for and leave. Now lead the way."

"I told you I don't have a safe. It's clear y'all have the wrong house. If you just leave now, we can forget all this even happened."

"I told y'all I wasn't here to hurt any of you. But if you don't take me to that fuckin' safe, I'm going to start killing y'all off one by one. Starting with him." Short Man pointed his gun at Philip, and Ava began to plead with him.

"Please! Please don't kill any of us. He's gonna show you where the safe is!"

Chance looked over at Ava and shook his head. Chance knew that the safe was the only leverage they had. Once it was opened, nothing was stopping the intruders from killing all of them. Chance wanted to protect everyone. He just needed Ava to allow him to do so.

"Show me to the fucking safe!"

'Tommy, baby, we never said we were killing anyone. You said this would be an in and out robbery. We already been in here past the time you said. We don't have any diamonds yet, and you talkin' 'bout killing them? This is not what you said would happen," the woman chastised, walking over to the shorter man they now knew was named Tommy.

"Damnit! Why the fuck would you say my name? I told you a hundred fuckin' times before we got here not to call me by my fuckin' name!" Tommy yelled. He was clearly upset.

"I'm sorry, baby," the woman whined"I got nervous and wasn't thinking. You started talking about killing people and it threw me off."

"Which way is the safe?" Tommy asked, ignoring the woman and turning back to Chance.

"It's on the third floor. In the library."

❧

CHOICE WALKED THROUGH THE HALLS CAUTIOUSLY WITH Chase at her side. They quietly made their way to Chase's room. "Get your phone, "Choice whispered. Chase nodded her head, walking over to her nightstand where her phone was sitting. She looked around, perplexed, before letting Choice know she couldn't find it.

"What you mean you can't find it?"

"I left it right here. I know I did because I put it on the charger, so I could watch TikToks tonight when Mommy and Daddy sent me to bed. And the charger's still right here." Chase held the cord up for Choice to see.

"One of them people probably took it," Choice replied, shaking her head in defeat. She thought for a moment before an idea popped in her head. "Where is your laptop?"

"It's in my closet, but you can't call the police from my laptop, Choice. We need a phone."

"Come on." Choice motioned. "I might not can call the

police, but I can send a DM to Brittani and tell her to call them."

They walked over to Chase's walk in closet and closed the door behind them. Choice grabbed the laptop from the shelf and opened it before having Chase put in her password. Choice downloaded Instagram, and the seconds it took to download felt like hours. Choice prayed silently that nobody would walk in and catch them while she attempted to get help. She also prayed that the rest of her family hadn't been hurt.

Once it was downloaded, Choice signed into her account before going directly to her messages. She went to the messages between her and Brittani. Once she found it, she opened it and began typing.

B, call the police. It's a bunch of people in my house with guns. They got my family, and me and Chase are hiding. Please hurry. I'm so scared.

Choice waited a few moments, heart pounding in her chest. She knew once Brittani saw the message, she would call the police. Choice just hoped she saw it in time. Several moments later, Brittani sent a reply.

OMG! Choice, my mama is on the phone with them right now. Do you know what they look like, or how many of them it is?

No, I don't know, but I know it's more than one, and they have guns. I don't know what they are doing to the rest of my family. Please tell them to hurry.

They on the way now. Stay hidden and don't make a sound.

Choice thanked Brittani before closing the laptop, letting Chase know help was on the way. Feeling safe in the closet, Choice informed Chase they should stay there until the police arrived, and she agreed. They sat on the floor, in the corner of the closet, waiting on their help to arrive. Choice finally felt a sense of hope, and she only prayed that her entire family would stay safe until the police arrived.

"How will we know when they get here if we stay in the closet?" Chase asked, looking over to Choice.

"Someone will come get us. But we not leaving this area until they do. I know as soon as the police get them people out the house, Mama and Daddy gonna come looking for us," Choice assured.

CHAPTER 7

"You're going to tell me where that library is," Tommy enforced, pointing his gun directly at Chance's head.

"He's going to show you where it is. Please just take that gun away from his head," Tamika pleaded. She was ready for them to leave and wanted them to do that without harming any of them. Tommy didn't say a word, only looked at Tamika with his gun still on Chance's head. Chance, not wanting to make any sudden movements, asked Tommy to follow him.

Tommy motioned for Deep Voice to come with him, and the three of them walked off down the hallway. Tamika scooted closer to Denzel, closing the gap between them. She looked at the woman and the tall man as they walked to the far corner of the room, whispering amongst themselves.

"Where is Choice and Chase?" Tamika whispered to Denzel.

"They ran off before anyone saw them. I don't know where they are."

"I hope they got away and went and got some help. But either way, we gotta figure out a way to get outta here. The longer we sit here, the less likely it is we gon' get outta here."

"You right about that. I can't just sit here and wait for them to kill us."

"I knew we should have drove here instead of flying. I couldn't bring my blicky on the flight."

"I like you." Denzel smirked. "What you think we should do?"

Before Tamika could answer, there was a hard knock at the door, followed by the doorbell. The woman offered to go to the door to see who it was before walking off.

"Nobody say a fucking word. If anyone makes a sound, I'ma shoot you right between the eyes," Tall Guy spoke.

"This could be our chance and our only one," Tamika informed.

"Corey, the police at the door." The woman came running back into the living room. She was breathing hard and shaking. Sweat began running down her face like a flowing river. Everyone in the room could see she was scared. Knowing the police were right outside made everyone feel better with everyone in the room knowing this robbery was coming to an end.

"Aisha, didn't Tommy just tell yo ass about using fucking names? Damn. Fuck is wrong with you?" Corey shot back.

"Who gives a fuck about them knowing our fucking

names when the damn police is at the door? I'm going to get Tommy. I knew this was a fucking mistake. We ain't even got the fucking diamonds. Now, we bout to be in prison for trying to commit a robbery. We ain't even got the shit yet."

"Calm the fuck down and go get Tommy and Brice. We gotta get the fuck up outta here," Corey ordered. "If any of you make a noise, I will shoot you. Try me if you fucking want to. I've already came here for nothing, and if I'm going to jail, I'ma go out like a fuckin' G." He spoke to everyone, but he looked directly at Ava, sending a cold chill down her body.

Remembering Chance saying they were going to the third floor, Aisha ran up the stairs two at a time. She wanted to get to Tommy as quickly as possible. She knew if nothing else, he would come up with a plan to get them out of there and away from the police. *I can't go to prison. I'm way too pretty for that shit.* She saw an opened door at the end of the hall and ran to it, hoping Tommy would be there.

"What the fuck you doing? I told you to stay downstairs. You left him alone with all them people? Are you trying to fuck the plan up?" Tommy asked, looking at Aisha when she walked in the room. Brice was standing at the safe with his gun pointed on Chance, trying to force him to open it.

"No, I'm trying to tell you that the police is already fucking up our plan because they at the door," Aisha notified. She was breathing heavy from running up the stairs, and she placed her hands on her knees, breathing in and out, trying to catch her breath.

"The police?" Brice asked. The look on his face let Chance know that he was nervous.

This is my chance to save my family. I gotta let the officers know we need help, Chance thought.

"Fuck!" Tommy yelled in defeat. He thought for a beat before coming up with a plan.

"Take him back downstairs," Tommy told Brice. "And if you alert the police in any way, I will kill the pretty wife and daughter you got right in front of you before they take me off to jail."

Chance nodded his head, letting Tommy know he understood before the four of them walked back down to the living room. The police were beating hard on the door, and Tommy knew they would need to move quickly if they still had a chance to get the diamonds and leave without being caught.

"Get the girl," Tommy ordered Aisha as he pointed to Chosen.

"Hell no! You are not taking my daughter anywhere," Chance interjected, stepping up to protect his child.

"Sit the fuck down before I blow yo fuckin' head the fuck off."

"Please don't take my daughter. Take me instead," Ava pleaded, standing to her feet.

"Don't worry. You going too," Tommy enlightened, grabbing Ava's arm. "You gonna answer the door and see what they want. Get them the fuck outta here. And to make sure you do, Aisha gonna have your baby girl. One fuck up and her pretty little brains will be all over the floor."

Tommy and Aisha took Ava and Chosen and walked them to the front door. Aisha took Chosen and stood off to the side, holding the gun to her head. Ava looked on, wanting to beat the shit out of Aisha for having a gun on her daughter.

"Wipe your face and open the door. Don't let them in, and if you alert them of what's going on, yo daughter is dead," Tommy spoke. He walked over to the door, standing off to the side with his back against the wall, so he would be behind the door when it opened. Ava nodded her head, taking a deep breath before opening the door.

"Good evening, Officers. Merry Christmas. How can I help you tonight?" Ava asked, looking at the officers with a smile on her face.

"Ma'am, is this your home?" one of the officers asked.

"Yes, it is. How can I help you?"

"We received a call stating there was a home invasion at this address."

"I'm sorry. A home invasion?" Ava chuckled. "I'm not sure who would have called you and said that. We are just wrapping up Christmas dinner."

"One of your daughter's friends called. Said your daughter sent a message to her on social media telling her it was masked intruders in your home with guns."

"I'm sorry, Officers, but I have no idea what you are talking about. We just in here having a regular Christmas dinner. In fact, I was just setting up the dessert table."

"Ma'am, the caller stated that your daughters were hiding

in the home away from the intruders. Are you sure you don't know what I'm talking about?" the officer asked.

"Officer, I can assure you my daughter is not hiding in the house from any masked intruders. This all sounds like someone playing on the phone if you ask me," Ava stated.

The officer stood there, looking into Ava's eyes for several moments, trying to detect a lie. "Ma'am, if you feel unsafe and feel like you can't verbally express what's going on, you can always give us a sign. Something like blinking your eyes or something like that. That would be a safe way to let us know something is wrong."

Ava looked at him, not blinking at all. Inside, she was screaming for the officers to come inside, arrest the intruders, and save them all. However, she knew she would have to stay calm, so instead, she stood on her word, telling the police nothing was wrong before watching them walk back to their squad cars. Ava's chest dropped as she watched their only hope for safety walk away. Before getting inside his car, the officer looked at the house once more, still seeing Ava standing at the door before closing it.

"You did good. Your daughter is still alive because of you," Tommy spoke, stepping up to Ava. He placed his gun to her face, and Ava felt the coldness of the steel against her skin. He slowly ran it down her face and over her neck before stopping at her chest. Aiming the gun directly at her heart. "If you want to keep your daughter alive, then you will tell us what the fuck that officer was talking about."

"I don't know. I was just as surprised as you were when

they came to the door. None of us called anyone. Y'all took our phones, so how could we?"

"Who else is in this house?"

"Nobody," Ava answered, tears streaming down her face.

"Then why are you crying?"

"Because you're holding a gun to my chest."

Grabbing Ava, he held his arm around her neck, turning her around and placing the gun on her head. He called for Aisha, and she stepped up into the entryway, her gun on Chosen.

"Who else is in this house?" he asked Chosen.

Ava looked at her with pleading eyes. Silently asking her not to say a word. She needed Choice and Chase to stay wherever they were until the intruders were out of their home.

"Answer my question or I will shoot her right now!" Tommy yelled, cocking his gun.

Chosen didn't know what to do. She didn't want to cause any harm to her sisters or to her mother. Tears ran down her cheeks as she became torn between the two.

"I told you nobody else was in the house. You already had yo man check it, and he said nobody else was here. The police either had the wrong house, or somebody was playing on the phone," Ava pleaded.

"Tell me now, little girl, because if I ask again, I'm going to kill her!" Tommy commanded.

"My two sisters might be in the house! I don't know. They ran off when y'all came in. I don't know where they are or even if they still in the house," Chosen informed.

Ava closed her eyes, saying a silent prayer for her two younger children, praying they'd gotten out the house. Opening her eyes, she saw Chosen mouthing the words, *I'm sorry*. She knew Chosen was afraid and didn't know what else to do. So, she wasn't upset. She just hoped they wouldn't be able to find Choice and Chase.

Tommy and Aisha walked Ava and Chosen back to the living room before forcing them back against the wall with the others.

"Baby, are you okay? They didn't hurt you, did they?" Denzel asked, wrapping his arms around Chosen.

"No, they didn't hurt me."

"Come with me to check the house. It's two other kids here," Tommy announced, looking over at Brice.

Chance looked over at Ava, and she just shook her head. Tears were streaming down her face as the fear of what might happen to her children became too much for her. Philip looked around at the masked men. Up until now, he'd been quiet, but he could no longer do so. He had to do as much as he could to protect his grandchildren.

"I'll go!" he spoke up.

"What?" Tommy asked, looking down at Philip in confusion.

"I'll go get them and bring them down here. They are just young girls and don't have anything to do with what's going on. Can you imagine how terrified they will be if two strange men just come to find them? Please just let me go. Y'all can even come with me." Philip was pleading with Tommy, now standing to his feet with his hands in the air. Tommy thought for a minute before turning back to Brice.

"Stay here with them. I'll take the old man with me."

"Are you sure, Tommy? I can go too," Brice suggested.

"Nah, I got it. If his old ass tries anything, I'll blow his fucking face off."

Brice nodded his head before watching Philip and Tommy walk out the room.

❧

"How long is it going to take for the police to get here? I'm scared, Choice," Chase asked, laying her head on Choice's shoulder. Choice should feel her shaking, and she wrapped her trying to comfort her. All they had to do was wait on the police, knowing they would all be safe once they arrived.

"They on their way. They might even be here. We just gotta wait for them to find us. Stay calm Chase, I promise everything is going to be okay."

"Can you message Brittani again and see if they said anything to her?"

Nodding her head, Choice stood to her feet, grabbing Chase's laptop before sitting back down. Getting back onto Instagram, she shot a quick message to Brittani. When Brittani replied back, telling Choice the police were sent away, she was beyond confused. *Why would they leave after getting a call there were intruders in the home?* She was just about to send

Brittani another message when the closet door flung open. Choice was just about to scream when she saw it was her grandfather. Chase smiled, standing to her feet and rushing over to him, but stopped when she saw one of the masked men walking in behind him. Choice looked at Philip, confused.

"Grandaddy, what's going on? Why did you come get us if they still here? Chase asked. Her little mind running a mile a minute. She couldn't understand why her grandfather had just brought the danger they were hiding from right to them.

"It's okay, y'all, but we gotta go downstairs," Philip spoke.

"But Granddaddy?"

"Listen to your granddaddy, little girl, and everything will be fine," Tommy encouraged.

Without any other choice, Chase and Choice walked out of the closet, heading to the living room with the rest of their family. Chase ran to her mother the moment she saw her, crying in her arms as Ava promised her everything would be okay. Choice walked over, sitting between Chosen and Ava.

"Are you okay?" Ava asked Choice, placing her hand onto hers.

"Yeah, I'm okay."

"So, y'all the little brave girls that called the police and almost killed your entire family, huh?" Brice said, looking between Choice and Chase. He walked up toward them, bending down before speaking again. "You pull anything like that again and I'm going to kill your little sister and make you watch." Choice's eyes widened. She believed everything he was saying.

"Get the fuck away from her. Do not talk to my fucking children anymore. I'm sick of this shit! Y'all came to get diamonds then let's go get some fucking diamonds, so y'all can get the fuck outta my house!" Chance had had enough. Seeing his young daughter crying and scared was enough for him. He walked up to Tommy, knowing he was the one in charge. He stared into his eyes, letting him know there was no fear in his heart. Tommy smirked, catching his message. Brice, seeing the potential threat, walked up to the two of them. He silently hoped Chance would jump stupid, and as soon as he did, he would knock him back down. Aisha, not listening to anything that was happening, stood with her back turned to everyone as she looked out the window. Corey stood on the other side of the room, pacing back-and-forth. Chosen looked around at everyone and thought this might be her only chance. Without drawing any attention to herself, Chosen got up and ran out the room. Aisha turned around just in time to see her running, but it was too late to stop her. She was just about to run after her when Tamika jumped up, grabbing her arm and stopping her from taking another step. Angela also jumped up, and before anyone could do anything, Angela punched Aisha in her face as hard as she could, causing Aisha to stumble backwards and fall to the floor. Corey, thinking quickly, ran off after Chosen. Philip, not wanting Corey to hurt his grandchild, ran after him.

This was it, the time they had all been waiting for. Denzel, seeing everything unfolding, stood to his feet. The moment he saw Brice grab Tamika, he went into action, running up and hitting Brice, causing him to drop his gun. Nate, thinking quick on his feet, grabbed the gun, but before he could aim it at anyone, Aisha fired two shots, one hitting Angela. Ava screamed as she watched her mother fall to the ground. Getting up from the floor, she rushed over to be by her side.

"Now dope that fucking gun and go back over there and sit the fuck down! Aisha yelled, aiming her gun at Nate. He quickly did as he was told and placed the gun onto the floor. Knowing that he would be shot before he could even raise the gun.

"Look at what the fuck y'all made me do! Why couldn't y'all just be cool? This shit was not supposed to go down like this!" Aisha yelled, waving the gun around frantically.

"Calm down, Aisha you did what you had to do. If you wouldn't of taken action they would have fucked up our entire plan. I know you didn't come this far to leave here with no diamonds," Brice consoled. Walking over to Aisha and placing both hands on her shoulders.

Nodding her head, she gave Brice a weak smile. Even though she knew he was correct, her pulling a trigger was never supposed to happen. She had a gun, yes. However she only carried it for the purpose of the robbery and was never supposed to use it. "Thank you for that, I'm good now," she replied, taking a deep breath.

Brice smiled at Aisha, before walking over to Denzel. Drawing back, he punched Denzel in the nose, causing it to bleed for a second time. "You lucky this all you got. I don't know a nigga that put they hands on me then lived to tell about it."

❦

CHOSEN HAD JUST GOTTEN TO THE DOOR WHEN SHE HEARD the shot. She stopped, hand on the knob, ready to turn around and see what was going on. She could hear her mother screaming. so she knew someone had been shot. Tears poured down her face, and her hands shook as she turned the knob.

"Chosen! Wait!" Philip called out.

Chosen turned around to see her grandfather standing there. Corey had his arm wrapped around his neck and was holding his gun to his head. "He's dead if you walk out that door," Corey spoke, causing Chosen to step away from the door slowly.

"Good girl! Now, walk yo ass back to the living room and sit the fuck down. And if you try that shit again, I'm going to kill everybody in that fucking room!"

Chosen dropped her shoulders in defeat, wishing she would have moved faster. She felt as though they would never get out alive. Every time a chance arrived it was intercepted and they were right back at square one. Tears formed in her eyes as Chosen dropped her head and began walking back to the living room.

CHAPTER 8

"She needs a doctor! We gotta get her to the hospital before she bleeds out!" Ava yelled as tears streamed down her face. Angela lay on the floor, blood pooling underneath her. She'd been shot in the shoulder, but there was so much blood that Ava knew it was bad.

"Ain't nobody going nowhere until we get what the fuck we came for. Now y'all gonna sit the fuck down. Y'all did this to her, not us. We told y'all to be fuckin' cool, and nobody would get hurt, but y'all just couldn't do that shit. Now this bitch bleeding everywhere!" Tommy yelled, clearly upset.

"She's going to bleed to death if we don't get her to a hospital now," Ava pleaded, sliding her mother over to the wall, not wanting her to continue laying in the middle of the floor. Knowing she wouldn't be getting to a doctor anytime soon, Ava looked around the room for something to stop the bleeding, knowing that if she didn't stop it quickly, it could deem to be fatal. Not wanting her mother to die, Ava became frantic, not being able to find anything to stop the bleeding.

"Here, you can take my sweater," Nate offered, removing his sweater and handing it off to Ava. She held it on the wound, pressing it tightly down on Angela's shoulder in an effort to stop the bleeding. However, the more she pressed, the more blood oozed out. Tears fell from Ava's eyes as she watched her mother bleed out. Ava didn't know what to do as she looked down at her mother helplessly.

"Oh, my God! Grandma!" Chosen yelled, rushing over to Angela the moment she walked back into the living room. Philip, seeing his wife against the wall, bleeding, did the same, rushing over to her and kneeling beside her.

"Oh, my God, Angela!"

"Don't worry, baby. I'm okay," Angela whispered weakly, looking over to Philip. "Don't worry."

"No, you're not okay, Mama. You've been shot," Ava replied, looking down at the hole in Angela's shoulder. Philip looked around at everybody in the room. He was clearly pissed and was ready to kill every one of the intruders one by one. Philip loved his wife, and the fact that she was lying here shot was not sitting right with him.

"Fuck! Y'all really shot her? I thought we wasn't gonna hurt anybody? Y'all said this would be an in and out hit. What happened to that? And y'all shot her? What if she dies? I can't go to jail for murder. Man, what the fuck?" Corey paced the floor, rubbing his hands over his head.

"Calm down, Corey. Ain't nobody going to jail. By the time anything happens, we gon' be long gone. The diamonds we 'bout to get gon' have us paid, and the lives we lived up until then won't matter anymore. So, just chill. Don't lose yo cool. That;s gon' fuck us up," Tommy reasoned.

"Calm down? None of that shit you saying matters if we get caught. Who gives a fuck if we got millions of dollars in diamonds if we in jail for fucking murder? We can't spend that shit behind the wall. We need to just leave while we still can. I didn't come here for all this."

"Leave while we still can? Fuck is you talking 'bout? Why do you think that's even an option? You sound crazy as hell if you think I'm leavin' here empty handed! Shut all that weak shit up so we can get this money!" Brice ordered, walking so close to Corey that their noses touched. Corey stepped back in an attempt to put space between him and Brice. Corey didn't want any problems. In fact, he was trying to avoid them, but Brice walked forward, wanting to let Corey know he meant what he said.

"Man, get out my face. I'm trying to be logical here, and the logical thing for us all to do now is to leave. We in over our heads. If we don't leave now, we gon' fuck around and end up in jail."

"You should listen to him. If she dies, all of y'all will go to prison. Even if y'all do make it out of here without getting caught, how are y'all gonna sell the diamonds? Have y'all even thought about that? I hope y'all don't think you can just take them to a pawn shop and shit gon' be sweet." Chance looked at Tommy, waiting for an answer. When Tommy didn't say a word, Chance knew he had him. "That is what you thought, huh? Well, I'm sorry to tell y'all, but you all have wasted your time. Each diamond has its own serial number that can be traced back to the owner. The moment you take any diamonds from this house to a pawn shop, you will be locked up. It's that simple. He's right. Y'all are in way over y'all heads."

"See what I mean? We ain't think this shit through." Corey shook his head.

"Man, why is yo scary ass listening to his ass? Can't you tell he lying? He gon' say whatever he thinks will stop us from taking his shit," Tommy assumed.

"Is that what you think I'm doing? Lying? Why would I lie at this point? I'm literally telling the truth. You can Google that shit if you don't believe me. Go ahead and fact check it now. Same way all money has a serial number, so does diamonds. I sign for each diamond right next to that number every time I buy them, which is a lot, so I think I know exactly what I'm talking about. So, y'all have one of two options. Y'all can choose not to believe me, take the diamonds, and go to jail, or y'all can let my family go and get my mother-in-law to the hospital."

"We need to choose the second option and get the fuck outta here." Corey spoke up.

"Nobody is going any fucking where. You gonna take me to them fucking diamonds is what's gon' happen. I think I'll just take my chances on going to jail. I knew I would be taking them chances the moment we walked into this house," Tommy decided, grabbing Chance and placing the gun to his head." Take me to that fucking safe."

"So, you just gonna pretend you didn't hear what the fuck he just said. You can't be serious? How much money is worth yo freedom? Bro, I'm out. Y'all do what y'all want, but I'm not about to stay here and continue to sacrifice my freedom. No money is worth me spending the rest of my life in jail for murder. Whatever happens after I leave is on y'all. I'm out," Corey spoke, putting his gun in his waistline as he began walking out the room.

"I'm only telling you once to get back here. You don't leave until we all leave. We came in together, and we all gon' leave together, and that's just what it is!" Tommy yelled out.

"Fuck that. Y'all dumb as fuck if y'all stay." Corey spoke the words with his back turned to Tommy as he continued walking.

Pow! Pow!

Without saying another word, Tommy shot Corey twice in the back, causing him to fall to the floor instantly. Both Choice and Chase screamed in fear from the shot, and they stared at Corey's body lying lifeless on the floor. Ava quickly crawled over to her daughters, wrapping her arms around them as they both cried. If the fear hadn't set in yet, it was now there for them all. Seeing Tommy kill one of his people without a second thought... the rest of them could only imagine what he would do to them. He gestured for Chance to follow him, and this time, he didn't protest, and he led him up to the library while the rest of them stayed inside the living room.

"Mommy, I'm scared," Chase cried.

"I know, baby. But Mommy and Daddy will never let anything happen to you. This will all be over soon. As soon as Daddy comes back, this will all be over," Ava assured, praying that what she was saying was true. However, the fact there was a dead body lying in the middle of her living room let her know things would never be the same again.

Nate looked around the room, knowing he needed to figure out a plan to get him and his family to safety. With one of the men dead and another with Chance, he figured this would be the time to make his move. He looked over at Brice, who was sitting on the couch, gun in hand. He knew Brice was the biggest threat, but if he could eliminate him, they would have a much better chance at getting away.

"Chosen, does your father have a gun in the house?" Nate whispered.

"Yeah, he does. He keeps in a lockbox in his closet, but I don't know the combination."

Okay, that's out. I ain't gon' have time to figure out no damn combination. Putting that idea to the side, he continued racking his brain.

"I see your brain workin', Nate. But don't do nothing that's gon' get you hurt," Tamika whispered.

"I gotta do something. Sitting here like this is what's gon' get us hurt. We gotta make a move."

"It's all about to be over. When Chance gives them the diamonds, they gon' leave," Angela spoke.

"They not though. As much as we all would love for things to end like that, I know it's not realistic. I watch too many true crime documentaries to fall for the bullshit. The truth is we were fucked the moment they got into the house. They gon' take them diamonds and kill us right after. We can take that shit sitting down, or we can try to fight our way out. Those our only options," Tamika proposed.

"They said they were not here to hurt any of us. They only want the diamonds," Philip spoke.

"Yet yo wife sitting here with a hole in her shoulder."

"She's right," Denzel agreed. "We gotta do something or else we gon' all die in here."

"I have to use the bathroom," Nate spoke up.

"Well, you're going to have to hold it," Brice replied.

"I can't, man. When you get to my age, your bladder just doesn't work like it used to."

"Then piss yoself, old man. I don't give a fuck."

"Aww, come on, man. I can't just sit here in my own pee. Let me just go to the bathroom," Nate pleaded.

"Come on, Brice. Just take him to the bathroom. Ain't nobody tryin' to sit here and smell old man piss."

Brice sat there, thinking for several seconds, before agreeing. "If you try anything, I'ma kill yo old ass."

"I just gotta go to the bathroom. That's it," Nate assured,

putting his hands in the air. They walked out the living room with Nate leading the way. Nate began walking up the stairs, but Brice quickly stopped him.

"Fuck you doin', old man? I know this big ass house got a bathroom on this level."

"This my son's big ass house. I'm just here visiting. I only know where the upstairs bathroom is. I just want to go handle my business. If I take the time trying to find another bathroom, we gon' have a real mess on our hands."

Nodding his head, Brice followed Nate up the stairs and down the hallway. When they got into the room, Nate walked over to the en-suite bathroom, locking the door behind him. Walking over to the sink, he leaned on it, using a few seconds to get his thoughts together. He didn't have a plan, but he knew he would need to come up with one quickly. *Come on, Nate. You gotta figure out something. Yo family is depending on this.* As if a lightbulb went off in his head, he looked over at his medicine bag. Nate had diabetes and was put on insulin shots as a result. Opening his bag, he pulled out three empty syringes before opening the cabinet under the sink. Just as he suspected, there was a host of cleaning supplies. Pulling out the bottle of Pine-Sol, he opened it before filling each one of the syringes. Placing the Pine-Sol back under the sink, he flushed the toilet, pretending he'd gone to the bathroom. Turning on the water, he washed off the syringes as well as his hands, washing away the smell of the Pine-Sol, placing the syringes into his pockets. He walked out the bathroom as if nothing was up, walking out the room with Brice right behind him.

"Thank you for that. I needed that release. My bladder felt like it was going to bust."

Brice didn't say a word. There was no need for small talk because he simply just didn't care. Walking back down the stairs, they walked back into the living room.

CHAPTER 9

Chance walked into the library, Tommy right behind him, gun on his head. Chance knew this was the moment of truth because the moment he opened his safe and Tommy saw there were really no diamonds inside, he knew all hell would break loose. Slowly, he walked over to the safe, trying to buy himself some time. "Are you sure you want to do this? If you go to prison, all this would be for nothing. Is that what you really want?" Chance was trying everything in a last attempt to save face.

"Open the fucking safe and stop playin' with me. Don't test me right now. I just killed one of my own people so shooting you would be nothing." Tommy cocked his gun. His patience was wearing thin, and he was ready to end it all if Chance didn't hand over the diamonds. Nodding his head,

Chance put in the code to the safe. Opening it, he stepped to the side, allowing Tommy full access to the safe.

Tommy smiled knowing he was about to be rich. Placing his gun in his waistline, he walked toward the safe. Chance studied his every move, trying to find the right time to make his move. He knew this would be his only chance, and if anyone had to sacrifice themselves for his family, it would be him. Inching closer, he tried to be as quiet as he could, not wanting Tommy to know he was behind him until it was too late. Chance's heart pounded with each step he took, and he prayed Tommy couldn't hear it. His hands began to sweat as nervousness set in. He wished he could go back in time. If he could, he never would have opened the door. He would have listened to Tamika when she said there wasn't a delivery man at the door on Christmas day. However, the reality was he couldn't change the past. Now he had to do everything he could to ensure his family had a future.

Chance wanted nothing more than for his entire family to be able to walk out of this alive. He took a step every time Tommy did, and when he made it to the safe and looked in, Chance made his move, snatching Tommy's gun and holding it on him before Tommy even knew what was happening. He turned around slowly with a sinister smile on his face, hands in the air, as Chance held the gun on him.

Do you even know how to use that, Mr. Diamond Dealer? You probably never held one of those in yo life. Punk ass, silver spoon nigga like you, you standing here in yo big ass house in yo designer clothes looking down on me. You think cause you got that gun in yo hands that you got one up on me, huh? Yo bitch ass ain't gon' shoot me, and I'm still gon' walk out of here with what I came here for."

"Shut up!" Chance yelled.

"Is my talking making you nervous? You not gonna shoot me, so give me back my fucking gun, and maybe I won't kill your entire family while you watch." Tommy was furious that he'd been tricked. Not only were there no diamonds, but Chance was now standing there holding his gun on him.

"Downstairs, now!" Chance ordered, still holding the gun.

Tommy nodded his head, hands still in the air. Taking a few steps forward, he pounced on Chance, wrestling with him for the gun. They rolled on the floor, each one of them trying to take control of the gun. Chance still had it in his hands and was trying his hardest not to let go. They struggled for several seconds before Chance finally took full control, placing his finger on the trigger and firing once.

The moment the gun went off, Tommy stopped struggling, falling alongside Chance. Chance jumped to his feet, gun still in hand. There was a hole in Tommy's chest, and blood poured from it as he struggled to breathe.

"Help me... I don't want to die," he spoke between breaths.

Chance said nothing as he looked down at Tommy, watching him bleed out. Chance had never killed anyone in his life, but the remorse for his actions were non-existent. Now armed, he knew he had the upper hand. Walking out of the library, he closed the door before walking down the hall, turning the corner that led him to the back staircase. With his pistol leading the way, he walked down the stairs slowly, not wanting anyone to know he was coming. Coming down the back stairs would allow him to sneak up on them, catching them all off guard.

❧

"DID YOU HEAR THAT? IT SOUNDED LIKE A GUNSHOT," Aisha asked, turning around to look at Brice.

"Yeah, I heard it too, I'ma go check it out," Brice informed. "Maybe we should just wait on Tommy to come back down." Aisha was already on edge after shooting Angela and didn't want anything else to happen. She felt if Brice left her alone they would overtake her. All she wanted was for Tommy to come back down with the diamonds so they all could leave.

"What if Tommy needs my help up there?"

"Nah, if anything the other guy needs help. We both know Tommy well."

Brice hesitated for several seconds before nodding his head, and agreeing with Aisha. "I'll wait for a few minutes, but if he don't come back down here soon, then I'm going up."

Ave became nervous, they'd all heard the shots, and she only prayed her husband was safe. She looked around at her family. Her children were all terrified, her mother was shot and she was almost certain Denzel's nose was broken. What started off as the dreamiest Christmas they'd ever had quickly turned into a nightmare. She felt so helpless as Choice and Chase cried in her arms. *How can I continue to tell them everything will be okay if I don't even believe it? It's a dead body in our living room. Ain't no way they gonna let us out of here alive.*

The room was so silent you could hear a pin drop as everyone waited for Tommy and Chance to arrive back downstairs. After several minutes of waiting, Brice informed Aisha once more that he was going to check on Tommy. Having heard the shot, and neither of them back down stairs yet, Brice was starting to get nervous. Aisha, realizing something could seriously be wrong, agreed.

"Sit on the couch, that way you can keep an eye on them all at once. If any of them try anything you better shoot or all this is for nothing," Brice coached.

Aisha nodded her head, fear written all over her face. She walked to the couch slowly, clearly not wanting to be left alone. She watched as Brice walked out of the room, his gun leading the way.

"I got a few syringes in my pocket. They're filled with cleaning solution. With her being by herself, this is probably going to be our only chance," Nate whispered to Tamika.

"How can we get close enough to inject it in her when she is holding a gun?

"I don't know, but we gotta figure it out, and we don't have a lot of time to do so. It's only her down here right now. So, this is the best time for us to go. We can do this, we just gotta come up with a plan, but we have to do it quickly."

Angela, hearing Nate and Tamika decided she would try to help spoke up. "I need to lay on the couch. This floor is hard and I'm losing so much blood, I just need to lay down."

Aisha looked over at her as if she was trying to decide what to say. She saw the blood that was still coming from Angela's shoulder, and although she'd been the one to shoot her, Aisha felt terrible about it. So, with that, Aisha nodded her head, agreeing for her to lay on the couch, standing up so she could be placed there comfortably. Nate and Philip both stood to their feet, helping Angela to hers. With Tamika standing up as well, offering to place extra pillows on the side of the sectional Angela was going to lay on. They all worked together to execute the plan they'd put in motion.

"They're in my right pocket," Nate informed, looking over at Tamika. They walked over to the couch slowly with Nate and Philip both on opposite sides of Angela. She was extremely weak from the massive amount of blood she'd lost, and they all knew they had to take this chance. If nothing else, to get Angela the medical attention she so desperately needed. Tamika placed several pillows at the end of the couch before Nate and Philip helped her sit down before laying her back,

"Tamika, can you put my legs on the couch for me? I'm too weak to lift them."

Walking over, she slipped her hand into Nate's pants pocket. Grabbing one of the syringes before picking up Angela's legs and placing them gently on the couch.

"Okay, y'all got her to the couch, now get ..." Before Aisha could say another word Tamika grabbed her. Placing her arm around her neck as she held the syringe to her jugular vein.

"What the fuck are you doing?"

"We bout to get the fuck outta here and you gonna let us or I'm going to pump this shit in yo fuckin veins," Tamika notified. "Y'all get up and go to the door."

"You go pump shit in my veins? Lady, let me go." Aisha was surprisingly calm, not even raising her voice.

"You can try me if you want to. I don't have anything to lose and everything to gain. Me and my family are about to walk out of here. And unless you want this shit in yo body, you not gonna stop us."

"Hahaha. It's funny you even think this is about to happen. Nothing is stopping us from getting these diamonds. If I'm dead when Tommy and Brice come back in here, what do you think will happen next? And since I'm not the only one in this room that wants the diamonds, y'all ain't gon' do shit to me."

Everyone stopped, looking over at Aisha, shocked. Her words had stunned them all as she'd just shined some light on a dark situation. Someone in that room had set it all up. The intruders were sent there by someone they cared about, and they all were in shock. Ava, needing to know what Aisha meant by her statement, walked over to her.

"What you mean you not the only one in this room that wants the diamonds. Somebody here sent y'all? Nah, I don't believe that. We are all family here, so I know you lying." she stated.

"Now, I know you smarter than that. How you think we know about everything? Who told us about the safe if it wasn't someone in this room? And if you think I'm lying, why don't you go ahead and ask Philip what I'm talking about."

The entire room looked over at Philip, mouths open, shocked at the revelation. None of them would have ever thought Philip would be the one to organize this entire robbery. Tears formed in Ava's eyes as she looked over at her father. The man who had loved and protected her and her mother her entire life. Now, he'd brought danger directly to her front door. Ava's heart broke as she looked into her father's eyes. The fact that she wasn't saying anything let Ava know what Aisha was saying was true.

"Chosen, you and Denzel get Choice and Chase and get outta here. Run to Brittani's house and call the police. Y'all will be safe there. Be careful and don't stop running until y'all get there." Ava spoke, needing to make sure that if nothing else, her children would be safe. Once they all ran out, she turned back to her father, looking for him to answer the questions she had.

Tears filled his eyes as he saw all the disappointment in his daughter's eyes. "Ava, I never thought all this would happen, you have to believe me. I would have never put you and the girls in any danger. You think I knew anything like this was going to happen? Your mother is sitting here with a hole in her shoulder. You have to know this was not how it was supposed to go."

"What! Philip, please tell me you're not serious. You did

this? Why would you do something like this Philip? Why?" Angela's eyes were pleading with her husband to tell her the truth. She would have never thought in a million years that her husband was capable of doing something so heinous.

"Because we are broke. And I'm not talking about the kind of broke to where I can still pay the bills. We are about to lose our house. I needed to come up with a quick way to make some money. And I know all of Chance's diamonds are insured, so I figured it wouldn't be much of a loss for him. I mean look at how y'all live. Y'all not wanting for anything and the insurance would pay for the stolen diamonds anyway. But it was never supposed to happen like this. They were only supposed to come in when y'all were not home. Get the diamonds and whatever else they wanted and leave. But then Ava, you informed me there was a safe in the house where all of the important things were kept. I knew there was nothing more important than the diamonds, so I knew they would be locked away in the safe. When I informed them, they let me know they had a way to get around it. What I didn't know was their plan was to come in here today, Philip explained.

"Daddy, you could have just let us know you needed money, we would have helped you and you know that. Why would you steal from us? Do you see what's happening? It's a dead body in my living room. My children will be scared for life after seeing that man shot dead right in front of them, and that's all yo fault. How could you do that? Is money the only thing that's important to you?"

"I'm sorry." Was all Philip could say.

Chance stood in the doorway, listening to everything that was being said. He knew it had to be an inside job, he just never thought Philip would be involved in any way. Walking into the living room, gun in hand he looked over at Philip in disgust. He wanted to shoot him right between the eyes for doing this to his family. The only thing that stopped Chance was the fact that Philip was Ava's father.

"Mom and Dad, y'all take my car and get Angela to a hospital. My keys are in the drawer by the front door." Chance spoke, walking over to Aisha, holding the gun on her so Tamika could let her go.

"Y'all won't make it out this house before Tommy and Brice come back down here." Aisha spat.

"Tommy is dead, so he won't be going anywhere but to hell. And when Brice comes back down, he can join Tommy," Chance replied.

Aisha's eyes widened at the mention of Tommy being dead. Not believing him, Aisha called Chance's bluff. "There ain't no way Tommy let you kill him. Do you know who Tommy is? Tommy a G, and he ain't 'bout to be taken out by some punk ass square like you."

"Think what you want, but that muthafucka laid out on my library floor and he ain't ever getting up.

"Put yo fuckin' gun down!" Brice yelled, rushing into the room gun pointing at Ava. "If you don't get that gun off of her right now, I'm gonna shoot yo wife.

"And if you do, I'm going to kill this bitch before turning

the gun on you," Chance shot back. The two men stood there, both waiting for the other to make a move.

"Brice, where is Tommy?" Aisha asked.

"He's upstairs, dead."

Before either of them could make a move, they all heard four words that changed their lives. "West Bloomfield Police Department!" the man called out. With those words, Brice quickly lowered his gun and attempted to run, but was quickly apprehended by two officers walking towards him. Aisha was also taken into custody right along with Philip. The officers led Chance and Ava out of the house and into an ambulance to get checked out.

The girls and Denzel pulled up a few moments later, with Brittani's father driving them back home. They all hugged their parents; happy they were both okay. Chosen looked over at one of the police cars and saw her grandfather sitting in the back of one. It crushed her heart to know he was the reason for all of this.

"Daddy, where is Grandma, Papa, and G mommy?" Chase asked.

"They went to go take Grandma to the hospital. Matter of fact, how bout we all get in the car and go to the hospital? We need to see how Grandma is."

Ava looked up at her house. The beautiful house that had been a home to her and her family for years. She looked at the beautiful Christmas lights she'd put up, hoping to have a wonderful Christmas and create a wonderful memory. Instead, what she saw was a horror house where her biggest fears had come true. Two monsters had died in that house, and Ava knew she could never call it home again. Even if the house was cleaned and remodeled , the memories of what had taken place would forever be in her mind. She looked over at her father one last time, shaking her head in disappointment. She knew nothing would ever be able to fix their relationship after this. There was no way Ava could ever trust him again and that hurt her to her core.

After giving their statements to the police, they all went to the hospital. Denzel was treated for his broken nose, while the rest of them went to check on Angela. Thankfully, the doctors informed them that she would make a full recovery. The family spent the rest of the night at the hospital, simply thankful they were all able to walk away with their lives.

CHAPTER 10

ONE YEAR LATER

It was the first Christmas in their new home, and Ava decided they would host again this year. The prior Christmas had been deemed to be a difficult one for their family, and they all vowed that this one would be ten times better. Their new home was a thousand square feet bigger than their last home, so Ava prepared herself and began decorating several days earlier. The entire house was decorated with red and gold décor. Beautiful poinsettias, both real and fake were all around the home, and there were hundreds of white lights all around. Ava was used to putting up two Christmas trees every year, however this year, she put up four. One on each floor, with the last one, a beautiful pink and white tree that was put in Chase's room per request.

The house was beautiful, and Ava couldn't have been happier with her work. Just like the year before, Chances and Ava's parents were coming to spend Christmas with them. The only difference was, that Philip was in prison on a ten year sentence for conspiracy to commit armed robbery. Angela filed for divorce the moment she was released from the hospital and refused to go to any of Philip's court dates. Ava however needed to know what would happen. Even though Philip was her father, she felt no remorse for him. So, when the judge handed down ten years, Ava was okay with that. Even feeling like he needed more.

Angela had moved to Michigan after her divorce and Chance and Ava vowed to take care of her. Buying her a condo about twenty minutes away from them and paying all of her bills. Life had been going good for the family the past year, and they all were excited to celebrate yet another Christmas together. This time without the intruders.

It was Christmas morning. Nate and Tamika had flown in the day before, while Angela had come to spend the night. They were all sitting around the living room. Fireplace lit and curtains open, watching the falling snow and the children sit around the tree opening their gifts. The smiles on their faces warmed everyone's heart as they unwrapped gift after gift. Ava sat on the couch sipping from her coffee mug as she watched her children. She was beyond grateful her family was here to celebrate yet another Christmas Day.

After all the gifts were open, Chosen walked up to her

room, putting away all her gifts, before heading back downstairs, helping her mother and grandmothers in the kitchen. Denzel was coming to Christmas dinner and Chance had been the one to invite him. Denzel had started spending more time with Chosen and her family for the past year. With him and Chance's relationship becoming one of a father and son. Chosen was happy and wouldn't change a thing. If it was one thing those intruders did was bring their family closer together.

Chosen went to her room, took her shower, and began getting dressed for the day. Turning on her playlist, she hooked her phone to her Bluetooth speaker. Mariah the Scientist's Aura began playing. She sang along as thoughts of Denzel entered her mind. Their relationship had grown over the past year, with them agreeing to move in together when Chosen turned eighteen next year. The love they had was real, and Chosen was happy everything had worked out in their favor.

Taking a seat at her vanity, Chosen applied her makeup, before removing her bonnet from her head and curling her hair. When she was done, Chosen dressed in a tan oversized Gucci sweater with a pair of brown Gucci stockings. After placing her tan, red bottom pumps on her feet and spraying herself with Kay Ali's Vanilla 28 she headed downstairs. She knew Denzel was on his way, so she went to the living room, joining her father and papa on the couch as they watched the game.

"You look beautiful, baby girl," Chance complimented.

"Thank you. I love the sweater, Papa. It goes great with my stockings. I was hoping I would get something to match them." Chosen smiled.

"You're welcome, Pumpkin, I was hoping you would like it. Can't be too sure about y'all kids and fashion these days. Shit goes out of style every two seconds." Nate laughed.

Chosen sat on the couch for several more moments before the doorbell rang. Knowing it was Denzel; she rushed to the door. Not wanting him to have to stand out in the cold. She wrapped her arms around him the moment he walked through the door.

"Merry Christmas, baby,"

"Merry Christmas. You look beautiful and you smell good as hell," Denzel complimented. Taking several sniffs from Chosen's neck.

"Thank you." She smiled. Being told she smelled good would always be Chosen's favorite compliment.

Chosen led Denzel around the house, allowing him to greet everyone before they made their way upstairs. Denzel handed Chosen her gift. A small box covered in a gold bow. Taking the bow from the box, Chosen opened it, mouth instantly dropping to the floor. "Denzel, what is this?"

Inside the box was a one-carat diamond ring. Her eyes widened as tears of joy formed in them. She looked over at Denzel and he had the biggest smile on his face.

"This is a promise ring. It's my promise to you that it will always be an us. Although we are too young to get married right now, I want you to know that is something that is going to happen. I am so grateful to have someone like you in my life, and I want you here for the rest of my life. I love you, Chosen." Denzel placed a soft kiss on her lips.

"I love you too, baby. And I want nothing more than to spend my life with you. This is beautiful and I love it. Thank you."

"You're beautiful and you deserve it. You deserve the world, and when I'm able, I'm going to give you just that."

"With you by my side, I already have the world," Chosen replied." It's your turn to open your gift now." Reaching down, Chosen handed Denzel a medium-sized red box. Opening the box to find a black and gold Versace robe, he wrapped his arms around Chosen tightly.

"Thank you so much, baby. I love it."

"You're welcome. Now we both have one. We gonna have to take some pictures together in our robes," Chosen suggested.

"For sure, and you make sure you flash that ring so them niggas know our shit is official."

"Dinner is ready everyone," they heard Ava call out.

They all gathered in the dining room, around the table as Chance said grace. He was beyond thankful to God after everything his family had gone through the past year, and he knew they were truly blessed. God had really rained his blessings down on his family and they kept coming. They all sat around the table, eating the delicious meal and enjoying the family. They were all very thankful they had indeed made it through *A Holiday Heist*.

The End.
Happy Holidays!

REVIEW

Did you enjoy the read?

Let us know how much by leaving us a review on Amazon and
Goodreads

OTHER BOOKS BY

URBAN AINT DEAD

Tales 4rm Da Dale

The Hottest Summer Ever

Hittin' Licks For The Holidays: Atlanta

Wet Dreams On Lockdown: The Nurse

How To Publish A Book From Prison

By **Elijah R. Freeman**

Despite The Odds

By **Juhnell Morgan**

Good Girls Gone Rogue

Good Girls Gone Rogue 2

By **Manny Black**

Hittaz

Hittaz 2

Hittaz 3

Hittaz 4

Hittaz 5

Coldhearted

Coldhearted 2

By **Lou Garden Price, Sr.**

Charge It To The Game

Charge It To The Game 2

A Summer To Remember With My Hitta

Snatched Up By A Hitta

Santa Sent Me A Real One For Christmas

Wet Dreams on Lockdown: The Unit Manager

Thug Me The Right Way 2

Thug Me The Right Way 3

Seizing A Gangsta's Heart For The Summer

Yours For The Taking

By **Nai**

A Setup For Revenge

A Setup For Revenge 2

Wet Dreams On Lockdown: The Librarian

By **Ashley Williams**

Trickin' on a Heaux for Christmas: A BBW Love Story

Homie Hoppin' For The Holidays

Wet Dreams on Lockdown: The Female C.O

Letters Of His Love

By **Telia Teanna**

The State's Witness

By **Chris Green**

IN The Streetz 4
By **Tron Hill**

Bandemic
By **Freshh Moneyy**

BOOKS BY

URBAN AINT DEAD's C.E.O

<u>Elijah R. Freeman</u>

Triggadale

Triggadale 2

Triggadale 3

Tales 4rm Da Dale

The Hottest Summer Ever

Murda Was The Case

Murda Was The Case 2

Murda Was The Case 3

Hittin' Licks For The Holidays: Atlanta

Wet Dreams On Lockdown: The Nurse

How To Publish A Book From Prison

STAY CONNECTED

Follow
Elijah R. Freeman
On Social Media
FB: Elijah R. Freeman
IG: @the_future_of_urban_fiction